A Purnell book
ISBN 0 361 03855 0
First published 1977. Reprinted 1987
Copyright © 1977 Express Newspapers plc
Printed by Purnell Book Production Ltd
Paulton, Bristol. A member of BPCC plc
Macdonald & Co (Publishers) Ltd
Greater London House, Hampstead Road
London NW1 7QX. A BPCC plc company

RUPERT
and the Hidden Lake

Illustrated by Colin Petty
Based on an original story by Frederick Chaplain

Purnell

6

CHAPTER 1

Rupert was feeling very excited as he and his Mummy and Daddy prepared to leave for a holiday by the sea. The little bear followed his parents into the taxi which was to take them to the station. Mr Bear told the taxi-driver that they were ready to leave, and they were soon on their way to Nutwood Halt.

"Won't it be lovely, Mummy," said the little bear. "I can't wait to paddle in the sea!"

At length the station appeared ahead of them. After Mr Bear had thanked the taxi-driver and paid their fare, Rupert helped to carry their suitcases to the ticket office. They bought their tickets and had just walked on to the platform when the train drew in.

"We were just in time!" laughed Mrs Bear.

Finding an empty compartment, Rupert helped Mr Bear to put their suitcases on to the luggage rack. After a few minutes the train moved off, and the little bear looked with interest at all the places they passed on their journey.

"There's the sea!" cried Rupert some time later, and after clambering off the train with their luggage they walked the short distance from the station to their hotel. Mr Bear had booked some rooms there, and they had a fine view over the bay from their balconies.

"When we've unpacked our clothes may we go for a walk along the beach?" begged Rupert. "The tide is going out, and we could collect some shells."

"Don't be so impatient, Rupert!" laughed
Mr Bear.

"I think that's a good idea," said his mother.
"A walk in the fresh air will do us good after
our journey."

The family quickly unpacked their clothes
and set off for the beach. Running ahead of
his parents along the sea-front, the little bear

spotted a telescope.

"Oh, Daddy, look!" he said. "Please may I
try it?"

"Yes, of course," replied his father, as he
searched in his pocket for the correct coin.
"Here you are."

"Thank you, Daddy," said Rupert, and inserted the coin into the slot. Then he placed his eye carefully to the telescope, and peered all round.

"It's marvellous," he said. "I can see right across the bay and out to sea. I can even see a ship on the horizon quite clearly."

Moving the telescope from side to side, Rupert continued gazing through it. Then he shouted, "Now I can see the lighthouse on that rocky headland."

Rupert stared through the telescope. "Well I never," he said breathlessly. "There's an odd-looking balcony and a sort of crane with a bell hanging from it at the top of the lighthouse. And I can see someone standing on the balcony! Do you suppose it's the lighthouse keeper?"

Suddenly the little bear gave a cry of astonishment.

"It's not the lighthouse keeper at all," he shouted. "It's the Wise Old Goat! Whatever is he doing there?"

Mr Bear took hold of the telescope and peered down it. "It certainly looks like him," he said.

"Oh, Daddy, let's hire a boat and go and see

11

him," pleaded Rupert. "I would love to know what he's doing in the lighthouse."

Mr Bear looked a little doubtful, but when Rupert reminded him what a good friend of theirs the Wise Old Goat was, his father agreed.

"Very well," he said. "I expect he'll be quite pleased to see some friends. We can hire a boat from the beach."

Mrs Bear decided to stay behind. "I think I'll sit on the beach and rest," she said. "I feel quite tired after our walk. Don't be too long," she called.

"Don't worry," replied the little bear. "We shall be back quite soon."

Rupert followed his father on to the beach, and they had soon hired a small motor boat from the friendly boatman to carry them to the lighthouse.

The little bear climbed into the front of the boat, and Mr Bear sat in the back to steer.

"Be careful," said the boatman, as he pushed them off.

As Rupert and his father drew near to the

lighthouse they saw the Wise Old Goat standing on the rocks waving to them.

"Ahoy there!" he greeted them. "This *is* a
surprise! I didn't expect to see any of my
friends from Nutwood!"

As soon as the visitors had landed, Rupert
told the Wise Old Goat how they had seen him
through the telescope standing on the balcony
of the lighthouse, and had come to investigate.

Their friend led them up the steep steps
into the lighthouse. "It's been empty for many
years," he said, "and I decided to buy it."

"But what for?" asked Mr Bear, perplexed.
"Is it to be a holiday home?"

"Not quite," smiled the Wise Old Goat. "I
am making a study of the sea, and this is an
ideal spot from which to do it. Follow me and

I'll show you my laboratory."

The little party climbed breathlessly up some narrow winding stairs to the top of the lighthouse. Then the Wise Old Goat led them into a round room filled with all manner of equipment.

"Here I have all I need for my study," he explained. "One of the things I am hoping to find is a rare sea fern which I think may grow in these waters. I have designed the diving bell outside to help me in my search. Come and look."

The group stepped out on to the balcony at the top of the lighthouse. Rupert felt rather dizzy, and held on tightly to Mr Bear's hand.

"Come over here," said the Wise Old Goat, pointing to the round, transparent object hanging from a crane on top of the lighthouse.

CHAPTER 2

"So that's what I could see through the telescope," murmured Rupert.

"This is my diving bell," explained the Wise Old Goat. "As you can see, it's very small. It's just big enough to take the Professor's servant, and he's going to help me in my work. In fact, he is due to arrive today for the first descent to the sea bed."

"How exciting," gasped Rupert. "Oh, I do hope you find the sea fern!"

Just as Rupert finished speaking the Wise Old Goat had to leave the little bear and his father to answer the telephone. He was gone for several minutes, and when he returned he looked quite upset.

"Oh dear," he said. "That was the Professor. His servant is ill and won't be able to come and help me today after all. He may be in bed for at least a week. Now all my plans will have to be cancelled."

Rupert had a sudden idea. "Why couldn't I help you?" he suggested. "The diving bell is too small to take a tall person. But I'm not very big. Couldn't I help with your sea study?"

The Wise Old Goat smiled at the little bear. "Well, that would certainly help me a great deal," he said. "But what does your father think?"

"Oh, Daddy, please let me help the Wise Old Goat," begged Rupert. "You know he will take care of me."

Mr Bear thought carefully for several minutes. "I suppose you will come to no harm," he decided. "But you must promise to be very careful."

"Oh, thank you, Daddy," beamed Rupert. Turning excitedly to the Wise Old Goat he said, "When can we begin?"

"At once, if you are ready," said his friend. "The sea is very smooth at the moment, so we should waste no time."

The Wise Old Goat returned to his laboratory, and by pulling some levers he lowered the diving bell on to the balcony. Then he handed Rupert some glass jars.

"Put these inside the bell," he instructed the little bear. "You can put the specimens from the sea into them."

At the Wise Old Goat's bidding, Rupert climbed into the diving bell and settled himself on the floor.

"You will find a small radio on the side of the bell," explained his friend. "I shall be able to talk to you through that, and give you instructions. Now, are you ready?"

"Yes," Rupert whispered, feeling rather nervous. "I think so."

The Wise Old Goat firmly closed the door of the diving bell and returned to his laboratory. As he pulled two huge levers on the wall, the diving bell was

19

hoisted over the railings of the balcony on the crane, and began slowly moving down towards the sea. While the bell sank gently below the surface of the water the Wise Old Goat pressed another switch, which shone a powerful light all around the bell.

"Goodness!" gasped Rupert. "I can see all sorts of fish swimming by in the light!"

As he gazed in astonishment at the sea creatures all around him, the little bear felt a slight bump, and the diving bell gently settled on the sea bed. Just then he heard the Wise Old Goat's voice over the little radio.

"Hullo, Rupert. Are you all right?"

"Oh yes," replied the little bear. "I'm seeing

all sorts of wonderful things!"

"Well now we can begin our study," said his
friend. "You will see two levers on the ceiling
of the bell. If you hold those you can move the
bell wherever you want. I will release the
diving bell from its cable, and you can start to
move it along the sea bed and look for the
fern. But be sure you keep within the range of

the light."

"Very well," replied Rupert. "I'm ready."
Holding on to the levers he felt the bell lift up
slightly from the sea bed and begin to glide
forward. The little bear peered intently out of
the bell, looking for the sea fern the Wise Old
Goat had described.

21

CHAPTER 3

Suddenly he caught sight of a clump of dark green foliage to his left. Steering the bell closer, he cried out, "I think I've found some of the fern!"

The little bear allowed the bell to sink on to the sea bed once again, and then excitedly told the Wise Old Goat of his find.

"I know already," his friend laughed. "I have been following you on a little television screen here in my laboratory! Now you must collect some specimens from that fern, Rupert. Open the sliding door in the bottom of the bell, and pick some."

Rupert hesitated for a moment, but the Wise Old Goat reassured him. "Don't worry. The sea will not come rushing into the bell," he promised.

The little bear obeyed, and was soon collecting several sprigs of the fern and carefully
depositing them in the specimen jars. Just as
he was completing his task he noticed that
some fish were watching him.

"Oh dear," thought Rupert to himself.
"They look very unhappy. I wonder what is
the matter."

Then the little bear saw an eel wriggling

into the bell through the sand underneath.

"Why do all the fish look so unhappy?" Rupert asked.

"It's because the sea is not as salty as it used to be," explained the eel, "and it makes us very uncomfortable. The only answer is to open King Neptune's store of salt water in his lake on Brine Island. We have already sent a messenger to the King to ask for permission."

Rupert was very upset to hear of these troubles, and asked the eel what he could do to help.

24

"Do you think your friend in the lighthouse might be able to assist us?" said the eel.

Rupert promised to tell the Wise Old Goat of the plight of the sea creatures, and the eel wriggled out of the diving bell and on to the sandy sea bed.

Just then Rupert heard the Wise Old Goat's voice over the radio. "I think you've collected enough fern now, little bear. It's time to come back to the surface. Steer the bell back to the cable."

Rupert closed the hatch in the bottom of the bell and, using the levers again, soon guided the bell back to the cable. The Wise Old Goat pressed a switch in his laboratory and the cable was automatically attached to the bell. Rupert felt the diving bell moving slowly upwards, and it soon broke through the surface of the water and was hauled back on to the balcony. The Wise Old Goat and Mr Bear were waiting for him.

"Well done, Rupert!" said the Wise Old Goat, as he opened the door of the bell. "That was first-class work. I'm delighted that you managed to find such fine specimens of the fern."

Rupert was very anxious to tell the Wise Old Goat about his conversation with the eel. When he had finished the story his friend said, "I couldn't quite hear what you were saying over the radio, but it sounded serious. Now we must try to help the sea creatures as soon as possible. Come with me."

The little party returned to the laboratory, and the Wise Old Goat quickly produced a map.

"Look," he said. "This is Brine Island. It's not to far from here. This patch of blue in the centre is King Neptune's hidden lake. I shall go there first thing in the morning and see if I can open the store of salt water and let it flood

into the sea and make it saltier."

Rupert was staring excitedly at the map. "Oh, please may I go too?" he begged. "After all, I met the eel, and I'd like to help."

The Wise Old Goat said that he would be glad to have the little bear to help him, provided that Mr Bear would allow him to go.

"Very well," said Mr Bear. "I'm sure our friend will make sure you come to no harm. And now I must be off to collect Mummy from the beach. She will wonder what has happened to us. I will come back tomorrow afternoon to take you back, Rupert."

The little bear and the Wise Old Goat pushed Mr Bear away from the rocks in the boat and stood waving to him.

"Goodbye!" cried Rupert. "I will see you tomorrow!"

After supper, the Wise Old Goat showed Rupert to a little room. "Here's your bedroom, Rupert," he said. "I've left you some spare night-clothes. I will call you early in the morning for our journey."

As Rupert was dropping off to sleep he was startled by a strange sound. "Something seems to be moving around the light-house," he thought. "I had better go and investigate."

The little bear pulled on his dressing gown and climbed the winding stairs to the balcony. To his amazement he saw some flying fish circling around the lighthouse. One of the fish flew right up to the little bear and dropped a necklace into his hand.

"We are King Neptune's messengers," said the fish. "the King has asked us to give you his emblem. If you show it to the guardian of the lake, he will allow you to open the lock gates. The King has given his permission for the salt water to be released into the ocean."

Rupert was delighted. "Oh, thank you," he said. "The sea creatures will be so happy if I can help to make the sea salty again."

When the Wise Old Goat woke Rupert in the morning, the little bear lost no time in telling him of his encounter with the flying fish.

"I think you should wear the necklace around your neck, Rupert," advised his friend. "Then the guardian of the hidden lake will know that we are not enemies. And now we must be off. I will show you our flying machines."

The Wise Old Goat disappeared into his laboratory and returned a few minutes later dressed in a flying suit, with a machine strapped to his back. He handed Rupert a smaller machine and some goggles.

"This is your flying machine, little bear. We

shall reach Brine Island in no time by this method. Follow me to the balcony."

When they reached the balcony the Wise Old Goat strapped the machine to Rupert's back, and told him how to use it.

"There are two armrests with a crossbar between them," he said. "All you do is twist the bar one way to go slowly, and the other way to go fast. It's very simple."

"It looks as if it will be great fun!" chuckled Rupert.

The pair started up the machines and quickly soared into the sky above the lighthouse.

"I feel like a bird!" cried Rupert.

The little bear quickly learned how to handle the flying machine, and kept close to the Wise Old Goat. They flew higher and higher, leaving land far behind, and soon Rupert could see nothing but sea beneath him. At length the Wise Old Goat shouted excitedly above the wind.

"Look! There's land ahead! Can you see it? That should be Brine Island, if I've followed the map correctly."

Rupert peered intently into the distance, and could just make out a faint strip of rocky coastline.

CHAPTER 4

As the pair flew on the little bear saw the outline of a desolate island. "It looks a very gloomy place," he thought to himself.

The Wise Old Goat flew towards the centre of the island, and then began to descend. "Look below you, Rupert," he shouted. "There's King Neptune's lake!"

Beneath him Rupert spotted an enormous stretch of water. Following the Wise Old Goat, the little bear flew down towards the surface, and the pair landed on a rocky ledge by the side of the lake.

"What an extraordinary place," murmured Rupert. "There doesn't seem to be anyone at all living on the island. Do you think we've made a mistake?"

Turning to him the Wise Old Goat said, "Throw a few stones into the water. If this is the hidden lake they won't sink because the water is so salty."

Rupert picked up a handful of stones and threw them into the lake. To his astonishment they remained on the surface. "We must have found the right place!" he laughed in delight.

"Now we must find the lock gates which hold the water in the lake," the Wise Old Goat told Rupert. "I think that is the direction we must take, little bear," he said, pointing towards one end of the lake.

The pair set off on their journey, but they found that the way was very rocky. The Wise Old Goat often had to climb to the top of steep rocks, and then pull the little bear up on the

end of a rope. "Be careful you don't slip, Rupert," he warned.

At length the friends scrambled down a rocky slope and saw a great wooden barrier some way ahead of them.

"That must be the lock gates," cried the Wise Old Goat. "Come on, little bear, we're nearly there now."

As the pair neared the gates Rupert noticed a curious disturbance in the water.

"What's that, I wonder?" he muttered.

The Wise Old Goat peered closely at the spot, and as he did so the disturbance grew greater, and the water began to churn and froth.

"There's something in the water, Rupert,"

cried the Wise Old Goat. "Quickly, fly up into the air again. We'll be safe from danger there."

The Wise Old Goat quickly started his flying machine and was soon hovering in the air above his little friend. "Hurry up, Rupert!" he shouted, as he watched the churning water.

The little bear turned on his machine, but found to his horror that it would not start. It made a sputtering noise and then stopped. Before Rupert had time to try to start the machine again a great figure rose out of the water in front of him. It had a huge shaggy head, and a tail shaped like a fish.

Trembling with fear Rupert gasped, "It's a merman. I do hope he doesn't hurt me!"

The Wise Old Goat hovered above Rupert, shouting to him to run away. "This way, Rupert," he called. "There's a gap between the rocks!"

But before the little bear could move from

the rocky ledge the merman had caught his leg.

"I am the guardian of the lake," the merman thundered angrily. 'Who are you that you dare to come to this island?"

Rupert anxiously began to explain about their mission, and was very relieved indeed when the Wise Old Goat flew down to the ground beside him.

"Leave my young friend alone," the Wise Old Goat ordered the huge merman. "Can't you see that he is wearing your King's emblem? King Neptune has given permission for us to open the lock gates and let the salt water run into a part of the ocean where the sea creatures are in desperate need of it."

The merman loosened his grip on Rupert's leg, and the little bear told him about his meeting with the eel on the sea bed.

"So you see," Rupert ended rather nervously, "we are only here to help the sea creatures."

The merman's anger died down as he heard the story. "I believe you, little bear," he said.

"That is indeed King Neptune's emblem you are wearing. This means that my work here has ended. Many years ago the King asked me to guard the hidden lake until its salt water was needed to replenish the ocean. Now my task is completed and I can return to my home in the ocean. I will open the lock gates for you," and the huge figure swam across to the barrier.

The two friends gazed in astonishment as

the merman pulled on the enormous wooden beams. Slowly the gates moved apart, and the salt water from the lake began gushing forth on its journey to the ocean. The merman rose up in the water once again, and his great voice boomed across to Rupert and the Wise Old Goat.

"Goodbye, my friends. I am returning to my

ocean home." His great body disappeared into the foaming water and he swam out towards the sea.

As the pair watched the merman swimming strongly away, the Wise Old Goat said, "Now we must devise a way of getting you home, little bear. Your flying machine is beyond repair, and mine isn't powerful enough to carry both of us."

He thought for a few moments and then had an idea. "I know just the thing," he smiled. "Would you collect some large leaves for me while I find some springy branches?"

Rupert was feeling rather puzzled, but he did as he was asked, and after collecting a bundle of the largest leaves he could find, he returned to the Wise Old Goat. His friend had found some branches and was busy lashing them together to make the framework of a shallow bowl.

"Now give me the leaves, Rupert," he instructed. The little bear watched, mystified, as his friend covered the branches with leaves and laced them together with creepers.

"Now you have a little boat to travel back in, Rupert!" smiled the Wise Old Goat. "Some islanders taught me how to make this. It's small, but quite strong enough to take a small bear like you."

Rupert and his friend carried the boat to the water beyond the opened lock gates. "As soon as we reach the sea, I will take you in tow," promised the Wise Old Goat. "But until then I shall fly above you, and make sure that you don't come to any harm."

Rupert felt quite anxious, but climbed into the craft. The Wise Old Goat pushed him out into the current formed by the salty waters escaping from the lake.

"Don't worry, Rupert," he shouted, "I'll be flying close to you all the time."

CHAPTER 5

Reaching the middle of the current from the lake, the little craft was tossed about in the surging waters. Rupert was feeling rather frightened, and crouched on the bottom of the craft, clutching the sides of the boat to prevent himself from being thrown overboard. He looked up and saw the Wise Old Goat hovering above him.

"Hold on tight, my friend," he called. "The waters will be calmer when we reach the ocean."

At that moment the flood swept down a narrow valley, and Rupert felt the spray from the tossing waves fall on to his back.

"Oh, I do hope the ocean isn't too far," he though. "I don't know how much longer I can cling on."

41

Looking up, the little bear could see the end of the valley ahead of him.

"Hold on tightly, Rupert," the Wise Old Goat called above him. "There are some dangerous rapids ahead."

Rupert clutched the sides of the craft even more tightly as it was swept through frothing waves and swirling currents. Just as he felt he could hold on no longer the waters suddenly became calm. Peering over the edge of the craft, Rupert saw the valley behind him and the great ocean ahead.

"Oh, thank goodness," he cried in relief. "We've reached the sea!"

"Yes," called the Wise Old Goat. "You were very brave, little bear. Now I can take you in tow. We shall soon be back at the lighthouse."

Hovering in the air, the Wise Old Goat lowered a rope to Rupert. The little bear fastened it securely to the front of the craft, and his friend increased the speed of his flying machine. As the little craft skimmed across the water, Rupert spotted a figure in the sea.

"It's the merman," he shouted. "Good luck with your journey!"

"Goodbye, my friends," replied the merman. "May you have a safe journey."

The sun was setting as the pair caught sight of the lighthouse in the distance. "There it is," sighed Rupert happily. "I do hope Daddy isn't worried about me. He said he would collect me this afternoon."

Nearing the rocks on which the lighthouse stood, Rupert spotted a motor boat in the distance.

"There's Daddy," he shouted. "Hooray! He's only just come to fetch me!"

The the Wise Old Goat flew down on to the rocks and pulled Rupert's little craft into the edge. The pair waited for Mr Bear to approach in the motor boat, and then helped him to clamber ashore. As he tied the boat securely to a rock, Rupert began to tell Mr

Bear all about their adventures. There was so much to tell that the Wise Old Goat had to finish the story for him.

"Well, it has all been worthwhile," smiled Mr Bear. "The currents in the ocean will soon spread the salt from the hidden lake, and the sea creatures will be happy again. What a very good start to our holiday!"

As Mr Bear was speaking two dolphins leapt up from the water around the rocks.

"Why, I do believe they are thanking us," laughed Rupert. "Look how happy they seem!"

It was time for Rupert and Mr Bear to return to shore. "Mummy will wonder where we both are," said Mr Bear.

Clambering back into the motor boat they waved goodbye to the Wise Old Goat, who was standing by the lighthouse.

"Goodbye," he called. "I will see you back in Nutwood!"

44

As they left the lighthouse far behind, Mr Bear noticed some flying fish in the distance.

"That's odd," he murmured. "They seem to be coming this way."

Just then Rupert remembered the emblem he was still wearing around his neck. He gave a cry. "Of course! They have come to collect King Neptune's necklace!"

As the fish drew nearer to the boat, Rupert removed the necklace and threw it high into the air. One of the fish caught it in his mouth, and then the whole group turned and flew towards the horizon.

When Rupert and Mr Bear reached the shore they found the boatman anxiously awaiting them. "I was afraid you were lost," he said.

Rupert recounted his adventures and the boatman stared in disbelief.

"Well, that beats the tallest fisherman's story I've ever heard!" he laughed.